Nainai   Emmy   Dad

For Jeremy, Rachel, Ellie, Emmett, Noah, and Ezra—
my favorite artists. —S. T.

For my late grandmother, who crossed oceans with
bravery to bring us here. I carry you with me. —J. W.

We thank Tara Cederholm and Anne Olney of the Brookfield Arts Foundation, Nancy Berliner of the Museum of Fine Arts, Boston, Charles Kim of Charlotte & Company, and Lynda Roscoe Hartigan, Kathy Fredrickson, Daisy Yiyou Wang, Rebecca Bednarz, Caryn M. Boehm, Liz Gardner, Claire Blechman, Whitney Van Dyke, Melissa Woods, Chip Van Dyke, Kathleen Corcoran, and Bethany McKie of PEM for their generous guidance and support.

The illustrations in this book were hand-painted in mixed media to resemble the textures and atmosphere of Yin Yu Tang.

Background on the Yin Yu Tang house is drawn from Nancy Berliner, *Yin Yu Tang: The Architecture and Daily Life of a Chinese House* (Tuttle, 2003).

Credits: pages 42–44: photo by Cheng Shouqi; courtesy of the Brookfield Arts Foundation; photo by Richard Gordon; photo by Peter Vanderwarker; photo by Marc Teatum; photo by Dennis Helmar

Library of Congress Control Number: 2019021206
ISBN: 978-0-8757-7239-4

First published in the United States of America in 2019 by Peabody Essex Museum, East India Square, Salem, Massachusetts 01970.

Distributed by Six Foot Press, Houston, Texas

Printed in Singapore

First edition, October 2019
2019 2020 2021 2022 / 10 9 8 7 6 5 4 3 2 1

Designed by Joan Sommers, Glue + Paper Workshop
Edited by Rebecca Bednarz, Peabody Essex Museum

This book is set in Supernett with hand-drawn lettering by Justine Wong

PIECE BY PIECE

Words by Susan Tan
Pictures by Justine Wong

Peabody Essex Museum
Salem, Massachusetts

Six Foot Press
Houston, Texas

Museums have always been a special place for Nainai and me. This summer, we visited a new one every week.

"*Wah*—very smart!" Nainai exclaimed when I recognized an artist's work by the way they swirled skies or dotted mountains.

"Follow me!" Nainai said when we found a painting that made us sigh. Together, we danced the lines we saw, gliding elegantly, twisting squiggly, moving like bursts of paint. You'd think that wouldn't be allowed in a museum, but with Nainai anything is possible.

Later we'd eat dumplings and draw our favorite paintings.
Nainai would open her special album and we'd look at
photographs from when she was small.

Now Nainai is back in China. That's where she lives.
She says part of her home will always be with us,
no matter how far away we are.
But I'm not so sure.

Before she left, Nainai made a blanket for me.

Some squares are blue, like water or sky. Others hold scraps of our precious things: a corner of Nainai's apron, my baby jacket, a sweater scented with her perfume. We stitched it together, one memory at a time, piece by piece.

I bring it with me everywhere.

Even places I don't want to be, like this museum.

Dad says there's something special here. He can't wait for me to see it. But how do I explain that without Nainai it's like I have a missing piece? I have our precious things and memories, but those aren't the same as having her.

So I decide not to listen, since no museum can be the same without her. I sulk instead of eating my cookie in the cafe. (Though I eat it when he isn't looking—because cookie).

When I finally get up, I realize—

My blanket!
It's gone!

I have to find it.

"We'll keep an eye out," a woman with bright glasses reassures me. "You go enjoy the museum."

But how can I? I have no Nainai,
no dancing, and now no blanket. It's like
nothing is the same since Nainai left.
I won't enjoy the museum, no matter
what anyone says.

I stop suddenly. In front of me is a
wall, smooth and white. We're
standing in the courtyard of a house,
a house like the one where Nainai
lived as a little girl.

"This house came all the way from
China." My dad takes my hand.
"Want to go in?"

The house is two stories high. Standing in the courtyard, I can feel the warm sun on my face.

I see a flash of blue in the room ahead. My blanket! But it's only a scrap of cloth nestled in a basket.

"Everything here is from the house or nearby communities," my dad explains.

The sewing kit is simple, just like Nainai's.
I imagine brushing my hand over the cloth.
I hear the snipping of scissors and the
laughter of women as they stitch.
Startled, I jump away.

I trail my dad. I'm not going to be interested in anything I see. But from a doorway, another bloom of blue catches my eye.

It's a curtain, not my blanket. I bend in close and I hear padded feet—a nainai pretending she can't find her grandchildren and puzzling loudly. But the giggles tell me they're under the bed.

In the folds of the curtain, I see the games Nainai and I used to play. I feel sad and turn away.

I see more blue in the kitchen and race inside. It's just a dishcloth, but it reminds me of Nainai's apron. I feel the warmth of the wood-fired stove and smell chili peppers sizzling.

Outside, children's feet run by and women's voices yell out, "*Sssh!* Not in front of the Kitchen God!"

Nainai had that rule too—you couldn't say anything bad in the kitchen. I always wondered why.

I want to ask my dad about it, but I remember I don't want to talk about Nainai. So I ask, "Can we make dumplings later?"

"Of course," he says and smiles. "They're my favorite."

"Really?" My eyes are wide. "Mine too!"

Upstairs, a flash of blue brings me to the reception room. "A space for worship," my dad tells me.

The blue and white pile on the floor isn't my blanket. It's a jumble of porcelain fragments, broken and cracked. The porcelain Nainai used every day was just like this, repaired and re-glued again and again, piece by tiny piece.

"Because it's well loved," I say. "Well, that's what Nainai always says."

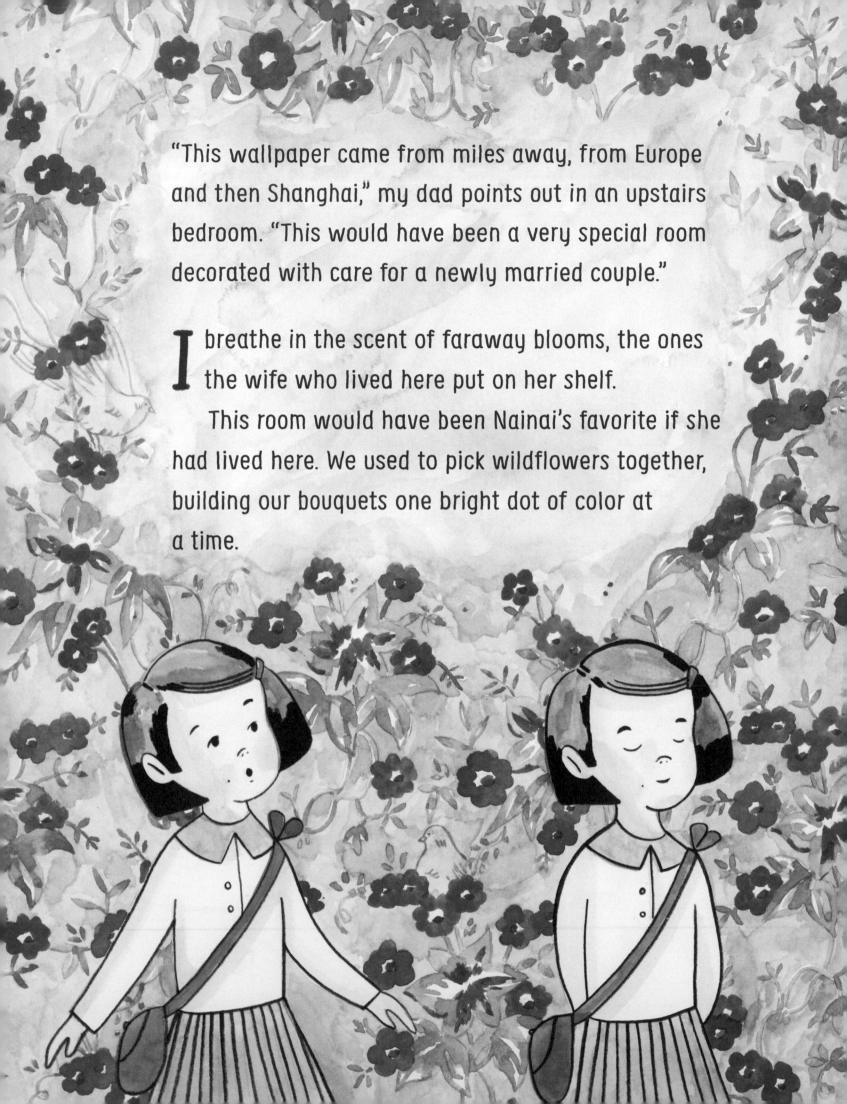

"This wallpaper came from miles away, from Europe and then Shanghai," my dad points out in an upstairs bedroom. "This would have been a very special room decorated with care for a newly married couple."

I breathe in the scent of faraway blooms, the ones the wife who lived here put on her shelf.

This room would have been Nainai's favorite if she had lived here. We used to pick wildflowers together, building our bouquets one bright dot of color at a time.

"Did the house really come all the way from China?" I ask.

"Like you and Nainai?"

"Like me and Nainai," he nods.

"Do you miss it?"

"Sometimes," he says. "But that's okay. Missing means you love something."

"It must have been hard," I reply, finally. "Bringing the house over, I mean."

"I think so. They took it apart and put it together, like a puzzle, piece by piece."

"And it fit back together?" I ask.

"Yes, after all that time and travel, it fit perfectly."

Downstairs, we peer inside a corner room. These rooms were for the older members of the family, each nainai and yeye.

A padded jacket rests on a chair as though someone's just left it there. It's just like the coat Nainai wears, the same blue I looked for when I'd follow her through a sea of paintings.

The feeling I get isn't just the past anymore but *now*. A powerful feeling of missing.

But that's okay.

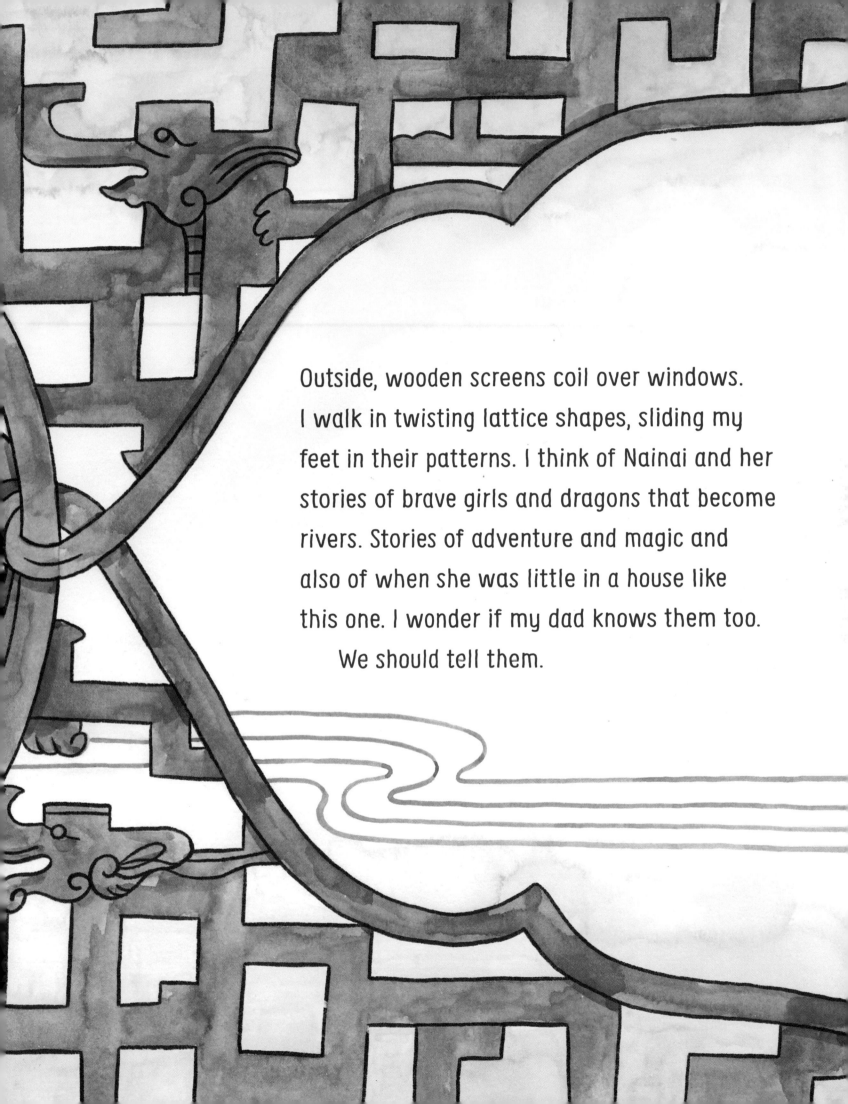

Outside, wooden screens coil over windows. I walk in twisting lattice shapes, sliding my feet in their patterns. I think of Nainai and her stories of brave girls and dragons that become rivers. Stories of adventure and magic and also of when she was little in a house like this one. I wonder if my dad knows them too. We should tell them.

Behind us, a fish splashes in the pool. My questions bubble up and this time I ask them.

"The water was here for safety," a smiling security guard says, "in case of fires."

"*Wah!*" I throw my arms wide, open like the pools. "Very smart!"

I feel the sun shining down on me and my smile beams the open sky. I twirl like the dragons on the window screens, winding and free. I soar like the sparrows in the courtyard, leaping up to peer over the edge of the pool.

I think of Nainai and anything's possible.

So when I turn to wave goodbye to the fish, I'm surprised, but not too surprised, when I see a flash of blue—

My blanket!

"How did we miss that?" My dad scratches his chin. My fingers trace the precious things my Nainai and I share, old and new.

The air changes. First one drop, then another. Rain falls in the open courtyard. The house fills with the warm smell of wood and water and home.

I turn to my dad. "Follow me!" I say.

No matter how far apart, we fit like a house put
back together, like squares stitched into a blanket,
like a perfect puzzle, piece by piece.

My dad and I hold my blanket around us like a clear
blue sky, like pooling water, like my Nainai's arms.

And together we fill the house with our dance.

YIN YU TANG, A SPECIAL CHINESE HOUSE

In the late eighteenth century, a prosperous merchant surnamed Huang built the house you see in these pages in a small village called Huang Cun in China.

Yin Yu Tang in the village of Huang Cun

The village is located in the mountainous Huizhou region, about 250 miles from the city of Shanghai.

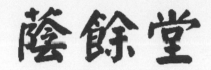

Yin Yu Tang in Chinese characters

The merchant called his elegant new home Yin Yu Tang, meaning "the hall of plentiful shelter." A man of literary and artistic taste, he designed a house with the hope of sheltering many future generations of his family.

Huang family members, about 1926

Ancestral Lines

Family lineage defines people in China. It is the essential bond between living people and their ancestors. For 200 years, one extended family, the Huangs, called Yin Yu Tang home. Eight generations lived in the home from the late eighteenth century until the 1980s.

At times, as many as three generations lived under its roof. The young men worked as merchants in cities a distance from the village in order to support their families. They undertook dangerous journeys to these cities and lived there for extended periods of time, sometimes for as long as six years. In their absence, women and the elderly were the primary residents of the house along with the children. While caring for the younger generation, they maintained the sixteen-bedroom home and raised their own vegetables and chickens.

Painted scenes and "horse heads" decorate the outer walls

The lush landscape of the village

Architecture and Decoration

Yin Yu Tang was oriented in the village according to the principles of the Chinese practice of *feng shui* to ensure a harmonious relationship with the landscape. Typically, Chinese homes face south, letting in sunlight and more *yang*, or masculine energy. Yin Yu Tang, however, was positioned toward the village waterways to the north with the green hills behind.

These geographical features made the unusual position of Yin Yu Tang more auspicious.

The bright white lime-plastered two-story house with its wooden post-and-beam structure, stepped end-walls (also called horse-head walls), and interior courtyard (or skywell) is typical of traditional homes in the Huizhou region. The decorative details—carved bricks and stones, painted scenes, and lattice windows—convey the aspirations and beliefs of the Huang family as well as the heritage of the region.

A phoenix represents a happy marriage and a vase is associated with peace

Yin Yu Tang is re-erected at the Peabody Essex Museum

The Big Move

Many ancient homes across China are being replaced with newer structures. In 1996, the Huang family descendants, who were living in other towns, decided that no one from their family would be returning to live in their ancestral village. In order to preserve Yin Yu Tang, the Huang family gave their blessing to move the house to the United States as part of a cultural exchange project with the local government.

A special team worked tirelessly over six years to carefully document, disassemble, label, pack, ship, and re-erect the house and its furnishings. With the guidance of curators, architects, structural engineers, stonemasons, carpenters, and timber frame specialists from the United States and

China, the house was researched, conserved, and restored. Yin Yu Tang, comprised of 2,735 wood components and 972 stones, was fit back together like a giant jigsaw puzzle on the Peabody Essex Museum grounds in Salem, Massachusetts. The house opened to the public in 2003.

The open skywell architecture of Yin Yu Tang

Yin Yu Tang Today

Yin Yu Tang gives us a special understanding of how historical and cultural changes in China affect individual people going about their daily lives. We invite you to visit the museum so you, too, can experience the wonder of Yin Yu Tang, rain or shine. Learn more at pem.org.